THE TALE OF
Peter Rabbit

THE TALE OF
PETER RABBIT

BY

BEATRIX POTTER

FREDERICK WARNE

FREDERICK WARNE

Published by the Penguin Group
Penguin Books Ltd, 80 Strand, London WC2R 0RL, England
Penguin Young Readers Group, 345 Hudson Street,
New York, New York 10014, USA
Penguin Group (Canada), 90 Eglinton Avenue East, Suite 700,
Toronto, Ontario, Canada M4P 2Y3
Penguin Ireland, 25 St Stephen's Green, Dublin 2, Ireland
Penguin (Group) Australia, 250 Camberwell Road,
Camberwell, Victoria 3124, Australia
Penguin Books India (P) Ltd, 11 Community Centre, Panchsheel Park,
New Delhi 110 017, India
Penguin Group (NZ), cnr Airborne and Rosedale Roads, Albany,
Auckland 1310, New Zealand
Penguin Books (South Africa) (Pty) Ltd, P O Box 9, Parklands 2121, South Africa

Penguin Books Ltd, Registered Offices: 80 Strand, London WC2R 0RL, England

Web site at: www.peterrabbit.com

First published by Frederick Warne 1902
This edition with reset text and new reproductions of Beatrix Potter's
illustrations published 2006

New reproductions copyright © Frederick Warne & Co., 2002
Original copyright in text and illustrations © Frederick Warne & Co., 1902
Frederick Warne & Co. is the owner of all rights, copyrights and trademarks
in the Beatrix Potter character names and illustrations.

Colour reproduction by EAE Creative Colour Ltd, Norwich

Printed in China

PUBLISHER'S NOTE

THIS EDITION, with reoriginated illustrations and type, marks the centenary of the first publication by Frederick Warne of *The Tale of Peter Rabbit* in 1902. Taking the first edition as a guide, the aim has been to follow faithfully Beatrix Potter's intentions while benefiting from advances in modern printing and design techniques. The colours and detail of the watercolours are here reproduced more accurately than ever before, and it has now also been possible to disguise damage that has affected the artwork over the years. The text is reset in a period typeface of the right weight to harmonise with the delicacy of the pictures. Most notably this edition restores six extra illustrations. Four of these (pages 10, 18, 49 and 62) were sacrificed in 1903 to make space for illustrated endpapers. The other two (pages 33 and 54) have never been used before, Beatrix Potter having initially prepared more illustrations than could be accommodated in the original format.

ONCE UPON A TIME there were four little Rabbits, and their names were —

Flopsy,
Mopsy,
Cotton-tail,
and Peter.

They lived with their Mother in a sand-bank, underneath the root of a very big fir-tree.

"Now, my dears," said old Mrs. Rabbit one morning, "you may go into the fields or down the lane, but don't go into Mr. McGregor's garden.

"Your Father had an accident there; he was put in a pie by Mrs. McGregor.

"Now run along, and don't get into mischief. I am going out."

THEN old Mrs. Rabbit took a basket and her umbrella, and went through the wood to the baker's. She bought a loaf of brown bread and five currant buns.

FLOPSY, Mopsy and Cotton-tail, who were good little bunnies, went down the lane to gather blackberries;

BUT Peter, who was very naughty, ran straight away to Mr. McGregor's garden,

AND squeezed under the gate!

First he ate some lettuces and some French beans; and then he ate some radishes;

AND then, feeling rather sick, he went to look for some parsley.

BUT round the end of a cucumber frame, whom should he meet but Mr. McGregor!

MR. MCGREGOR was on his hands and knees planting out young cabbages, but he jumped up and ran after Peter, waving a rake and calling out, "Stop thief!"

PETER was most dreadfully frightened; he rushed all over the garden, for he had forgotten the way back to the gate. He lost one of his shoes among the cabbages,

AND the other shoe amongst the potatoes.

AFTER losing them, he ran on four legs and went faster, so that I think he might have got away altogether if he had not unfortunately run into a gooseberry net, and got caught by the large buttons on his jacket. It was a blue jacket with brass buttons, quite new.

PETER gave himself up for lost, and shed big tears; but his sobs were overheard by some friendly sparrows, who flew to him in great excitement, and implored him to exert himself.

MR. McGREGOR came up with
a sieve, which he intended to pop
upon the top of Peter; but Peter
wriggled out just in time, leaving
his jacket behind him,

AND rushed into the tool-shed, and jumped into a can. It would have been a beautiful thing to hide in, if it had not had so much water in it.

MR. McGREGOR was quite
sure that Peter was somewhere in
the tool-shed, perhaps hidden
underneath a flower-pot. He
began to turn them over carefully,
looking under each.

Presently Peter sneezed —
"Kertyschoo!" Mr. McGregor
was after him in no time,

AND tried to put his foot upon Peter, who jumped out of a window, upsetting three plants. The window was too small for Mr. McGregor, and he was tired of running after Peter. He went back to his work.

PETER sat down to rest; he was out of breath and trembling with fright, and he had not the least idea which way to go. Also he was very damp with sitting in that can.

AFTER a time he began to wander about, going lippity — lippity — not very fast, and looking all round.

He found a door in a wall; but it was locked, and there was no room for a fat little rabbit to squeeze underneath.

AN old mouse was running in and out over the stone door-step, carrying peas and beans to her family in the wood. Peter asked her the way to the gate, but she had such a large pea in her mouth that she could not answer. She only shook her head at him. Peter began to cry.

THEN he tried to find his way straight across the garden, but he became more and more puzzled. Presently, he came to a pond where Mr. McGregor filled his water-cans. A white cat was staring at some gold-fish; she sat very, very still, but now and then the tip of her tail twitched as if it were alive. Peter thought it best to go away without speaking to her; he had heard about cats from his cousin, little Benjamin Bunny.

HE went back towards the tool-shed, but suddenly, quite close to him, he heard the noise of a hoe — scr-r-ritch, scratch, scratch, scritch. Peter scuttered underneath the bushes.

BUT presently, as nothing happened, he came out, and climbed upon a wheelbarrow, and peeped over. The first thing he saw was Mr. McGregor hoeing onions. His back was turned towards Peter, and beyond him was the gate!

PETER got down very quietly off the wheelbarrow, and started running as fast as he could go, along a straight walk behind some black-currant bushes.

Mr. McGregor caught sight of him at the corner, but Peter did not care. He slipped underneath the gate, and was safe at last in the wood outside the garden.

MR. MCGREGOR hung up
the little jacket and the shoes
for a scarecrow to frighten the
blackbirds.

PETER never stopped running or looked behind him till he got home to the big fir-tree.

HE was so tired that he flopped down upon the nice soft sand on the floor of the rabbit-hole, and shut his eyes. His mother was busy cooking; she wondered what he had done with his clothes. It was the second little jacket and pair of shoes that Peter had lost in a fortnight!

I AM sorry to say that Peter was not very well during the evening.

His mother put him to bed, and made some camomile tea; and she gave a dose of it to Peter!

"One table-spoonful to be taken at bed-time."

BUT Flopsy, Mopsy, and
Cotton-tail had bread and
milk and blackberries for
supper.

THE END

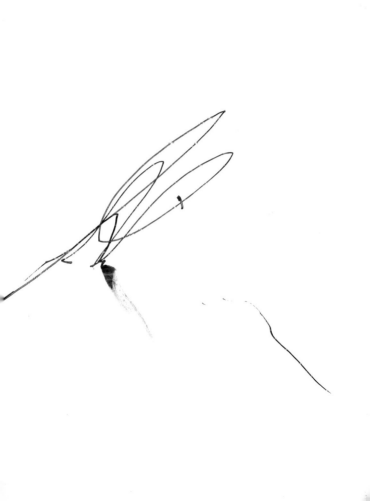

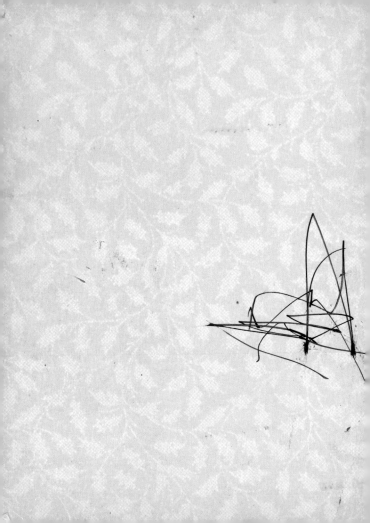